Richard Scarry's Mother Goose Rhymes and Nursery Tales

A GOLDEN BOOK · NEW YORK

Golden Books Publishing Company, Inc. New York, New York 10106

 Library of Congress Catalogue Card Number: 98-84345   ISBN: 0-307-30501-5   A MCMXCVIII

Contents

Richard Scarry's
NURSERY
TALES

LITTLE RED RIDING HOOD

Once upon a time there was a little girl. She was called Little Red Riding Hood because she always wore a red cape with a hood.

Little Red Riding Hood lived with her mother in a little house on the edge of a deep dark forest.

One day her mother said to her, "Your grandmother is not feeling well. I want you to take her some goodies."

She gave a basket of cookies and cakes to Little Red Riding Hood and said, "Don't dawdle along the way. I want you home before dark."

Little Red Riding Hood put on her red cape with the hood and set out through the woods to visit her grandmother.

As she was skipping along the path, a wolf suddenly stepped out from behind a tree. Little Red Riding Hood was so frightened she almost dropped her basket.

But the wolf smiled and said in his sweetest gruff voice, "Where are you going, little miss?"

"I am taking some goodies to my sick grandmother," answered Little Red Riding Hood.

"And where does your grandmother live?" asked the wolf politely.

"In a little white cottage in the middle of the forest," replied Little Red Riding Hood.

"Ah," said the wolf, "I know that house."

"I hope your grandmother will be feeling better soon," he called, slinking back behind the trees.

Little Red Riding Hood went on her way.

5

When Little Red Riding Hood was out of sight, the crafty wolf ran with all his might, by a short-cut, to Grandmother's house. He wanted to get there first.

He arrived breathless at Grandmother's house and knocked on the door.

"Who is there?" called Grandmother.

"It is I, Little Red Riding Hood," said the wolf, trying to make his rough voice sound soft.

"Just pull the latch string and come in, my dear," said Grandmother.

The wolf came in!

He leaped at Grandmother and swallowed her whole!

Then that crafty fellow put on a nightdress and a nightcap and climbed into bed to wait for Little Red Riding Hood.

"She will think I am her grandmother," he chuckled to himself.

In a minute there was a knock at the door.
"Who is it?" called the wolf, trying to sound like Grandmother.
"It is I, Little Red Riding Hood," answered the little girl.
"Just pull the latch string and come in, my dear," said the wolf.
Little Red Riding Hood came in and put her basket down.

"Come closer, my dear," said the wolf.
"Why Grandma, what big ears you have!" said Little Red Riding Hood.
"All the better to hear you with, my dear," said the wolf in his best grandmother voice.

"And Grandma, what big eyes you have!" the little girl said.
"All the better to see you with, my dear," said the wolf.

"And Grandma," said Little Red Riding Hood, "what big teeth you have!"

"All the better to EAT you with, my dear!" howled the wicked wolf.

Then he leaped out of bed and tried to grab Little Red Riding Hood.

But Little Red Riding Hood was too quick for him. She ran out the door screaming for help.

A sturdy woodchopper who was nearby rushed after the wolf and conked him on the head. The wolf fell dead.

8

Then the woodchopper noticed that something was moving around inside the wolf.

He cut the wolf open and out popped Grandmother. She was all right, but a little bit upset by her experience. It was a good thing the wolf was so greedy that he had swallowed her whole!

The woodchopper carried Grandmother back to her bed. Then they all had a snack from Little Red Riding Hood's basket of goodies.

Grandmother thanked the woodchopper for saving their lives, and kissed Little Red Riding Hood good-bye.

Then the kindly woodchopper took Little Red Riding Hood home — just in time for her supper.

THE GINGERBREAD MAN

Once upon a time a little old woman and
a little old man lived in a little old house.

One day the little old woman decided to
make a gingerbread man.

She cut him out of dough and put him
in the oven to bake.

After a while, the little old woman said
to herself, "That gingerbread man must
be ready by now."

She went to the oven door and opened
it. Up jumped the gingerbread man, and
away he ran, out the front door.

As he ran he shouted,
"Run, run, as fast as you can.
You can't catch me,
I'm the gingerbread man!"

The little old woman ran after the gingerbread man,
but she couldn't catch him.

He ran past the little old man
who was working in his garden.
"Run, run, as fast as you can.
You can't catch me,
I'm the gingerbread man!
I've run away from a little old woman,
and I can run from you, I can!"

The little old man ran, but he
couldn't catch the gingerbread man.

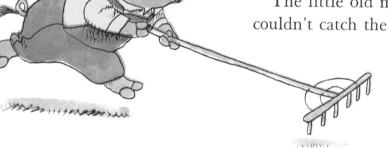

The gingerbread man came to a field of
mowers. He called out as he went by,
"I've run away from a little old woman,
and a little old man,
and I can run from you, I can!"

11

The mowers ran after him . . .

. . . but they couldn't catch him.

The gingerbread man ran on until
he came to a cow.
"*Run, run, as fast as you can.*
You can't catch me,
I'm the gingerbread man!
I've run away from a little old woman,
a little old man,
and a field full of mowers,
and I can run from you, I can!"

The cow ran . . .

. . . but she couldn't catch him.

13

He ran between two picnicking bears.
*"I've run away from a little old woman,
a little old man,
a field full of mowers,
and a cow,
and I can run from you, I can!"*

The bears jumped up
and ran after him.

14

They ran,

and ran,

but they couldn't catch
that gingerbread man.

15

Soon the gingerbread man came to a fox
lying by the side of a river, and he shouted,

"Run, run, as fast as you can.
You can't catch me,
I'm the gingerbread man!
I've run away from a little old woman,
a little old man,
a field full of mowers,
a cow,
and two picnicking bears,
and I can run from you, I can!"

But the sly fox just laughed and said,
"If you don't get across this river quickly,
you will surely get caught. If you hop on
my tail I will carry you across."

16

The gingerbread man saw that he had no time
to lose, so he quickly hopped onto the fox's tail.

"Oh!" said the fox. "The water's getting
deeper. Climb up on my back so you won't
get wet."
And the gingerbread man did.

"Look out!" said the fox. "The water's even
deeper. Climb up on my head so you won't
get wet."

And the gingerbread man did.

"It's too deep! It's too deep!" cried the fox. "Climb up on my nose so you won't get wet!"

And the gingerbread man did.

Then, with a flick of his head, the fox tossed the gingerbread man into his mouth. His jaws snapped shut . . .

18

. . . and that was the end
of the gingerbread man!

THE THREE LITTLE PIGS

Once upon a time there were three little pigs. When they were old enough they left their home to seek their fortunes.

Mother Pig was very sad to see them leave.

The first little pig met a farmer with a load of straw.

"Please sir," he said, "will you give me some straw to build a house?"

The farmer gave the first little pig some straw.

And the little pig built
a house of straw.

Along came a wicked wolf and knocked
on the door.

"Little pig, little pig, let me come in,"
said the wolf.

But the little pig answered, "No, no!
Not by the hair of my chinny, chin, chin."

"Then I'll huff and I'll puff and I'll blow
your house in," said the wolf.

And he huffed and he puffed
and he blew the house in,
and he ate the little pig up.

The second little pig met a woodcutter with a bundle of sticks.

"Please sir," he asked, "may I have some sticks to build a house?"

The woodcutter gave him some sticks and the second little pig built his house of sticks.

Then along came the wolf who said, "Little pig, little pig, let me come in."

"No, no! Not by the hair of my chinny, chin, chin," answered the second little pig.

"Then I'll huff and I'll puff and I'll blow your house in," said the wolf.

And he huffed and he puffed, and he huffed and he puffed, and he blew the house in, and ate the second little pig up.

The third little pig met a bricklayer with a load of bricks.

"Please sir," he asked, "may I have some bricks to build a house?"

The bricklayer gave him some bricks and the third little pig built his house of bricks.

Then along came the wolf who said, "Little pig, little pig, let me come in." And the third little pig answered, "No, no! Not by the hair of my chinny, chin, chin."

"Then I'll huff and I'll puff and I'll blow your house in," said the wolf. So the wolf huffed and he puffed and he huffed and he puffed.

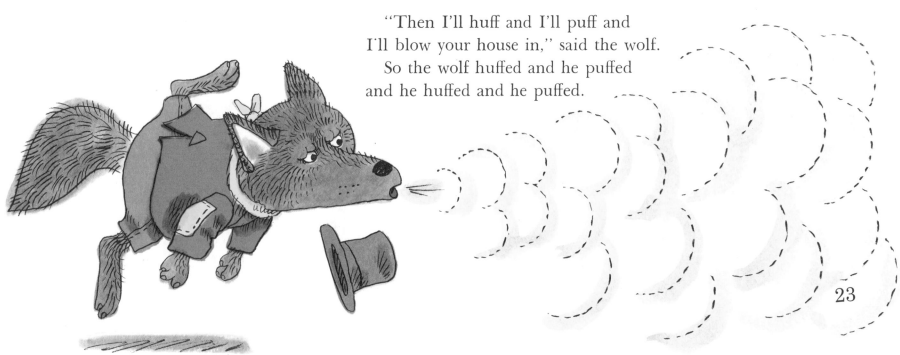

23

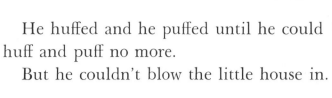

He huffed and he puffed until he could huff and puff no more.
But he couldn't blow the little house in.

"I must think of a trick to get that little pig out of his house," the crafty wolf said to himself.

After thinking for a while he said, "Little pig, I know of a garden where there are some tasty turnips. Will you join me at seven o'clock tomorrow morning and we will go and get some?"
"Where are they?" asked the little pig.
"Down in Misty Meadows," said the wolf.
The little pig agreed to go.

But instead of waiting for the wolf to come at seven o'clock, the little pig went at six o'clock all by himself, and brought home a full basket of turnips.

24

When the wolf came at seven o'clock he asked the little pig if he was ready to go.

"Why I have been there already," said the little pig, "and have brought home a full basket of turnips for dinner."

The wolf was very angry at this, but he pretended not to be.

He thought of another trick. "Little pig, I know where there is a nice apple tree," he said.

"Where?" asked the little pig.

"Over at Windy Hill," said the wolf. "I will come for you at six o'clock tomorrow morning and we will go together to pick some juicy apples."

Well, the little pig got up at five o'clock the next morning and went to the apple tree, hoping to get back home before the wolf came.

But it took him a long time to get there.

He was still up in the tree when he saw the wolf coming.

He was very frightened.

The wolf stopped under the tree and said, "Little pig, you got here before me. Are they nice apples?"

"Yes," said the little pig. "I will throw one down for you to taste."

But he threw it so far that while the wolf ran to catch it, the little pig climbed down and ran home.

The next day the wolf came to the little pig's house again. "Little pig, there is a fair at Shanklin this afternoon. Will you go with me?" he asked.

"Oh, yes," said the little pig. "When shall I meet you?"

"At three o'clock," said the wolf.

So the little pig, as usual, went earlier. At the fair he bought a butter churn to make butter in.

As he was going home with it he saw the wolf coming up the road. He didn't know what to do.

He decided to climb into the churn to hide.

But the churn tipped over and rolled down the hill.

The wolf was so frightened by it that he ran away home without going to the fair to find the little pig.

Now when the wolf found out that the little pig had been inside the churn, he was furious.

He went to the little pig's house.

"Little pig, little pig," he called, "you got away from me at Misty Meadows, Windy Hill, and the Shanklin Fair, but you can't get away from me now. I am coming down the chimney to eat you up!"

Well, the little pig quickly took the lid off the big pot of water on the fire . . .

SPLASH! Into the boiling water fell the wolf!

The wolf jumped up and ran howling out the door, never to return to the little brick house where the little pig lived happily ever after.

28

GOLDILOCKS AND THE THREE BEARS

Once upon a time there were three bears who lived in a little house in the woods.
Father Bear was a great big bear.
Mother Bear was a medium-sized bear.
And Baby Bear was a wee tiny bear.

One day Mother Bear made hot porridge for breakfast.
She poured it into their bowls and they all went for a walk in the woods while it cooled.

While they were gone, a little girl named Goldilocks came to their house.

She looked in the door and didn't see anyone there, so in she went. Now that was not right. She should have waited for someone to come home.

Well, Goldilocks saw the porridge on the table and suddenly felt very hungry.

She tasted the porridge in Father Bear's great big bowl. But that was too hot!

She tasted the porridge in Mother Bear's medium-sized bowl. But that was too cold!

Then she tasted the porridge in Baby Bear's wee tiny bowl. And that was just right! So she ate it all up.

Then she decided to sit down for a rest.
She sat in Father Bear's great big chair.
But that was too high!

She sat in Mother Bear's
medium-sized chair.
But that was too wide!

Then she sat in Baby Bear's
wee tiny chair.
And that was neither too high
nor too wide, but just right!

But the wee tiny chair was
not strong enough and it broke
all to pieces.

Then Goldilocks felt a little sleepy so she decided to go upstairs and take a nap.

First she lay down in Father Bear's great big bed.
But that was too hard!

Then she lay down in Mother Bear's medium-sized bed.
But that was too soft!

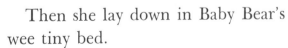

Then she lay down in Baby Bear's wee tiny bed.
And that was just right!
She snuggled under the covers and was soon fast asleep.

Pretty soon the Bears came back from their walk.

Father Bear saw a spoon in his great big porridge bowl.

"Someone has been tasting my porridge," said Father Bear in his deep gruff voice.

Mother Bear saw a spoon in her medium-sized porridge bowl.

"Someone has been tasting my porridge," she said in her medium-sized voice.

"Someone has been tasting my porridge," said Baby Bear in his wee tiny voice, "and has eaten it all up!"

Then Father Bear noticed that the cushion was not straight on his great big chair.

"Someone has been sitting in my chair," he roared in his deep gruff voice.

Mother Bear noticed that the cushions on her medium-sized chair were all mussed up.

"Someone has been sitting in my chair," she said in her medium-sized voice.

"And someone has been sitting in my chair and has broken it all to pieces," said Baby Bear in his wee tiny voice.

Then the three bears went upstairs to
see what they would find there.

"Someone has been sleeping in my bed,"
said Father Bear in his deep gruff voice.

"Someone has been sleeping in my bed,"
said Mother Bear in her medium-sized voice.

"Someone has been sleeping in my bed,"
said Baby Bear in his wee tiny voice,
"and here she is!"

When Goldilocks heard Baby Bear's wee tiny voice, she awakened in a fright. She jumped up out of the wee tiny bed, scrambled down the stairs and ran out of the house. And she didn't stop running until she got home.

And she never again went to the house of The Three Bears.

THE WOLF AND THE KIDS

Once upon a time a mother goat and her seven little kids lived in a cozy house near a deep forest. And in that forest lived a wicked wolf.

One day, Mother Goat had to go shopping. She called her children to her and warned them, "Lock the door and do not open it to anyone while I am gone, for it might be the wicked wolf who will want to eat you up."

The seven kids promised not to open the door to anyone and Mother Goat went on her way.

Shortly after she left, there was a knocking at the door.

"Let me in, my dear children," a voice said. "It is your mother and I have brought something for each of you. Open the door and let me in."

The seven kids were ready to open the door when they saw a black paw on the windowsill.

"You are not our mother!" they cried. "Our mother's paw is white and yours is black. You are the wicked wolf! Go away!"

So the wicked wolf went to the baker and said, "Cover my paws with white flour or I will eat you up."

The poor baker was very frightened so he did as he was told.

The wolf went back to the cozy house near the forest and put his white paw on the windowsill.

"Open the door, my dear children," he said. "It is your mother and I have brought something for each of you."

The seven kids saw the white paw. "It's Mother!" they cried and they opened the door.

In bounded the wicked wolf!

The kids were terrified and ran to hide.

The first ran under the table.

The second sprang into bed.

The third hid in the laundry basket.

The fourth jumped into a barrel.

The fifth climbed into a cupboard.

The sixth crawled under a washtub.

And the seventh and youngest got into the grandfather clock.

But the wolf found them and popped them all into his sack — all but the youngest who was in the grandfather clock. Then that wicked wolf started back home through the forest.

The sack was so heavy that he soon had to stop and lie down for a rest. And he dozed off, dreaming of the fine supper he would have.

When Mother Goat arrived home, everything was topsy-turvy.

And her children were nowhere to be found!

Then she heard a noise in the clock. Out jumped the youngest kid who told his mother how the wolf had tricked them all.

Mother Goat set out to find the wolf and soon she came upon him snoring under a tree. She saw something moving in the sack.

The rope around the sack was so tight she couldn't untie it, so she rushed home to get her sewing basket. She took her scissors and snip! snip! snip! she cut open the sack.

One, two, three, four, five, six! Out bounded her little kids.
Mother Goat told each of the kids to find a big stone. She filled the empty sack with them and neatly sewed it shut.

41

After a while the wicked wolf woke up. He threw the sack over his shoulder and started off again.

"My this sack is heavy," he said. "What plump little kids I have caught."

The wolf was very hungry by the time he had carried that heavy sack all the way home. He opened it up right away.

"What!" cried the wolf. "Stones?"

He was very angry, and very disappointed, and very very hungry. So he packed his things, went home to his mother for supper, and never came back again.

THE MUSICIANS OF BREMEN

Once upon a time, Donko Donkey decided to
go to the town of Bremen. Once he was there
he hoped to become a town musician.

As he walked down the road he met
Davy Dog and stopped to chat.

"Where are you going?" asked Davy Dog.

"I am going to Bremen to become a
town musician," Donko replied.

Davy then and there decided that
he would like to do that, too.

So off they went together on the
road to Bremen.

As they walked along they sang a happy duet, braying and barking together.

Kitty Cat heard them and ran to meet them. "Where are you going?" she asked.

When Donko and Davy told her, she decided that she wanted to be a town musician, too.

So off they went singing a trio.

They had not gone far when they met Rocky Rooster. When he found out what the three musicians were going to do, he asked, "May I join you? I can sing too, cock-a-doodle-doo."

They welcomed him and so there were four musicians on their way to Bremen.

But the town of Bremen was far away.
The dark night came and they lost their
way. They were tired from their long walk,
and very hungry.

Then, off in the distance, they saw a
light shining in the window of a house.

"Perhaps there we will find something
to eat and a place to sleep," said Donko.

"But we must first make sure that the
people are friendly," said Rocky.

So they crept silently up to the house.
Donko, who was the tallest, peeked in
the window.

"What do you see?" asked Kitty Cat.

"Why, I see four robbers!" exclaimed Donko. "They are sitting around a table enjoying a great feast. And lying around the room are all kinds of things which they have stolen."

"We must think of a plan to chase the robbers away," said Davy.

The musicians were all very hungry and would have liked to be enjoying that feast themselves. The food didn't belong to the robbers anyway, for they had stolen it. So the four musicians thought of a plan.

Davy jumped up on Donko's back.
Kitty climbed up on Davy's back.
Rocky perched on Kitty's back.
Then, Rocky began to crow,
Kitty began to meow,
Davy began to bark,
and Donko began to bray.

You never heard such an awful racket in all your life!

47

The robbers jumped up out of their chairs in terror! They thought some monster was about to eat them.

Out the door and into the forest they ran, as fast as they could go.

The four musicians went in and finished eating the robbers' supper. My, but it tasted good!

48

Then they turned off the lights
and lay down for a good night's sleep.

Meanwhile, about midnight, the robbers
saw that the house was dark and quiet.
"We should not have been scared so
easily," said Grumbuff, the chief robber.
"One of us must sneak back in to see if it
is safe for us to return."
Grumbuff was too scared to go himself,
so he told Snaggle-Tooth Louie to go.

49

Trembling with fear, Snaggle-Tooth Louie entered the pitch-dark house.

He was fumbling about trying to light a candle when he tripped over Kitty Cat and woke her up. Kitty leaped up and scratched him.

Scared out of his wits, Snaggle-Tooth Louie ran to the door, where Davy bit him in the leg and Donko gave him a kick.

Rocky woke up and started crowing — "Cock-a-doodle-doo!"

Snaggle-Tooth Louie ran back to his gang in the forest.

"We must flee!" he cried. "There is a terrible gang of horrible creatures in the house! A witch flew up and scratched me. An ogre stabbed me with a knife.

A giant hit me with a club, and all the time someone was screeching, 'Kill the robber, do!'"

The four robbers quickly turned and ran away. They never went near that house again.

The four musicians were so pleased with the house, they decided to stay there.

And should you ever go by that way, you will probably hear sweet songs coming from the window as the four friends sing their merry tunes.

51

THE THREE BILLY GOATS GRUFF

Once upon a time there were three Billy Goats Gruff.
One day they wanted to eat some berries which grew on
a hill across the river from where they lived. To get to the
hill they had only to cross over a bridge.

But under this bridge lived a big, bad troll.

TRIP-TRAP, TRIP-TRAP, the youngest Billy
Goat Gruff started to cross over the bridge.

"Who trips over my bridge?" roared
the troll.

"Only Littlest Billy Goat Gruff," said
the little goat.

"Aha! I am coming up to eat you,"
said the troll.

"Oh, don't eat me," cried Littlest Billy
Goat Gruff. "My brother is coming after
me, and he is much bigger."

So the troll let Littlest Billy Goat Gruff
cross the bridge.

Soon, TRIP-TRAP, TRIP-TRAP, the second
Billy Goat Gruff started to cross the bridge.
"Who trips over my bridge?" roared the troll.

"Only the Middle-Sized Billy Goat Gruff,"
said the second goat.
"Aha! I am coming up to eat you," said the troll.
"Oh, don't eat me," cried Middle-Sized
Billy Goat Gruff. "My brother is coming
after me, and he is much bigger."
So the troll let the Middle-Sized Billy
Goat Gruff cross the bridge.

Soon, TRIP-TRAP, TRIP-TRAP, the biggest
Billy Goat Gruff started to cross the bridge.
"Who trips over my bridge?" roared the troll.
"It is I, Great Big Billy Goat Gruff," said the biggest goat.
"Aha! I am coming up to eat you," said the troll.
"Come along, then," said Great Big Billy Goat Gruff.
So up came the old troll.

Well! Great Big Billy Goat Gruff put down his head and butted that ugly troll right off the bridge and he was never seen again.

Then the three Billy Goats Gruff ate those delicious berries until they grew so round and plump they were scarcely able to walk home again.

54

THE THREE WISHES

Once upon a time, there was a poor woodcutter who
lived with his wife in a humble cottage.

One day he said to himself, "I work hard all day but I never
earn enough money to buy all the things that we want."

A beautiful fairy overheard him.

She said to the woodcutter, "I will grant you three wishes,
but choose them carefully as you may have no more than three."

Then, in a wink, she disappeared.

The woodcutter hurried home to tell
his wife about their three wishes.

She was very happy as she thought
about all the things she would
like to have.

There were so many things they wanted, they couldn't decide what to wish for.

"Let us think about it some more before we wish," said the woodcutter as he sat down to a bowl of soup for supper.

"Oh dear," he said, "soup for supper again. How I wish I could have a nice fat sausage for a change."

And just like that, there was a nice fat sausage in his dish.

His wife was furious.

"Look what you've done!" she shouted. "You have wasted a wish on a foolish old sausage. How could you be so stupid? Now we have only two wishes left."

She kept on complaining until the woodcutter became so sick of hearing about the sausage that he shouted without thinking, "Oh, I wish that the sausage was stuck on the end of your nose!"

And, lo and behold, the sausage jumped to the end of her nose and stuck fast.

"Now look what you've done!" she cried. "You've wasted another wish. Get this sausage off my nose!"

They tried to pull the sausage off but it would not come unstuck.

"Well, we still have one wish left," said the woodcutter. "Let's think about what to wish for."

"What's there to think about?" cried his wife. "I can't go around with this sausage hanging from my nose. I wish this sausage would go away."

In a wink, the sausage disappeared. And so after their three wishes, the woodcutter and his wife were no better off than before. They didn't even get to eat the sausage for supper. Dear, oh dear!

THE TEENY-TINY WOMAN

Once upon a time there was a teeny-tiny
woman who lived in a teeny-tiny house.

One teeny-tiny day the teeny-tiny woman
put on her teeny-tiny shawl and went out
of her teeny-tiny house for a teeny-tiny walk.

She walked for a teeny-tiny time until
she came to a teeny-tiny church. She
opened the teeny-tiny gate to the teeny-tiny
churchyard and went in.

Inside the teeny-tiny churchyard, the teeny-tiny woman found a teeny-tiny bone. The teeny-tiny woman said to her teeny-tiny self, "This teeny-tiny bone will make some good teeny-tiny soup for my teeny-tiny supper."

So she put the teeny-tiny bone in her teeny-tiny pocket and went back to her teeny-tiny house. She went up her teeny-tiny stairs to her teeny-tiny bedroom.

She put the teeny-tiny bone into her teeny-tiny cupboard and closed the teeny-tiny doors.

Then, as she was a teeny-tiny bit tired, she got into her teeny-tiny bed to have a teeny-tiny nap.

She was asleep only a teeny-tiny time when she was awakened by a teeny-tiny voice from the teeny-tiny cupboard saying, "Give me my bone!"

The teeny-tiny woman was a teeny-tiny bit frightened so she hid her teeny-tiny head under the teeny-tiny covers and went to sleep again.

A teeny-tiny bit later the teeny-tiny voice cried out, a teeny-tiny bit louder, "GIVE ME MY BONE!"

This made the teeny-tiny woman a teeny-tiny bit more frightened and she hid her teeny-tiny head a teeny-tiny bit more under the teeny-tiny covers.

The teeny-tiny woman was asleep again for a teeny-tiny time when the teeny-tiny voice from the teeny-tiny cupboard called out a teeny-tiny bit louder,

"GIVE ME MY BONE!"

The teeny-tiny woman was even a teeny-tiny bit more frightened, but she stuck her teeny-tiny head out from under the teeny-tiny covers and said in her loudest teeny-tiny voice,

"TAKE IT!"

And that is the teeny-tiny end of this teeny-tiny story.

This little pig went to market.

This little pig stayed at home.

This little pig had roast beef.

This little pig had none.

And this little pig cried,
"Wee, wee, wee, I can't find my way home."

Once upon a time a Pig, a Cat, a Duck, and a Little Red Hen lived together in a little house. The Pig, the Cat, and the Duck were all very lazy and would never help with the work around the little house.

So the Little Red Hen had to do everything all by herself.

One day as the Little Red Hen was raking in the yard, she found some seeds.

"Who will help me plant these grains of wheat?" she asked.

"Not I," said the Pig.

"Not I," said the Cat.

"Not I," said the Duck.

"Then I will do it myself," said the Little Red Hen. And she did.

63

Soon the wheat grew tall and golden.
"Who will help me cut the wheat?" asked
the Little Red Hen.

"Not I," said the Pig.

"Not I," said the Cat.

"Not I," said the Duck.

"Then I will do it myself,"
said the Little Red Hen.
And she did.

When the grain was cut and ready to be ground into flour, the Little Red Hen asked, "Who will help me take the grain to the mill?"

"Not I," said the Pig.

"Not I," said the Duck.

"Not I," said the Cat.

"Then I will do it myself," said the Little Red Hen. And she did.

When the flour came back from the mill
the Little Red Hen asked, "Who will help
me make this flour into bread?"
"Not I," said the Pig.
"Not I," said the Cat.
"Not I," said the Duck.

"Then I will do it myself,"
said the Little Red Hen.
And she did.
She made the flour into dough.
She rolled the dough into a loaf,
and put it into the oven to bake.

When the loaf was baked she took it
out of the oven.
Mmmmmm! Didn't it smell good!

66

"Who will help me eat this bread?"
asked the Little Red Hen.
"I will," said the Pig.
"I will," said the Cat.
"I will," said the Duck.

"Oh no you won't!" said the Little Red Hen.
"I found the seed. I planted it. I harvested it.
I took the grain to the mill. I made the flour into bread.
And none of you would help me. I did the work all by
myself and now I am going to eat the bread all by myself."
And she did.

Richard Scarry's

Best MOTHER GOOSE Ever

Ring a ring o' roses,
A pocket full of posies,
A-tishoo! A-tishoo!
We all fall down.

List of First Lines

Little Boy Blue,
   Come blow your horn!
The sheep's in the meadow,
   The cow's in the corn.

Where is the little boy
   Tending the sheep?
He's under the haycock,
   Fast asleep.

Will you wake him?
   No, not I;
For if I do,
   He's sure to cry.

73

Bobby Shafto's gone to sea,
    Silver buckles at his knee;
He'll come back and marry me,
    Bonny Bobby Shafto!

Bobby Shafto's fat and fair,
    Combing down his yellow hair;
He's my love for evermore,
    Bonny Bobby Shafto!

Tom, Tom, the piper's son,
Stole a pig and away did run.
The pig was eat, and Tom was beat,
And Tom went crying down the street.

London Bridge is falling down,
    Falling down, falling down.
London Bridge is falling down,
    My fair lady.

Build it up with wood and clay,
    Wood and clay, wood and clay,
Build it up with wood and clay,
    My fair lady.

One misty, moisty morning,
When cloudy was the weather,
I chanced to meet an old man
Clothed all in leather.
Clothed all in leather,
With cap under his chin.
How do you do, and how do you do,
And how do you do again?

There was an old woman who lived in a shoe.
She had so many children she didn't know what
    to do.
She gave them some broth without any bread,
    scolded them soundly and sent them to bed.

83

Simple Simon met a pieman,
    Going to the fair;
Says Simple Simon to the pieman,
    Let me taste your ware.

Says the pieman to Simple Simon,
　　Show me first your penny;
Says Simple Simon to the pieman,
　　Indeed, I have not any.

85

Hickety, pickety, my fine hen,
She lays eggs for gentlemen;
Gentlemen come every day
To see what my fine hen doth lay.
Sometimes nine and sometimes ten,
Hickety, pickety, my fine hen.

Diddle, diddle, dumpling, my son John,
Went to bed with his trousers on;
One shoe off, and one shoe on;
Diddle, diddle, dumpling, my son John.

I do not like thee, Doctor Fell,
The reason why I cannot tell;
But this I know, and know full well,
I do not like thee, Doctor Fell.

There were once two cats of Kilkenny,
Each thought there was one cat too many;
So they fought and they fit,
And they scratched and they bit,
Till, excepting their nails
And the tips of their tails,
Instead of two cats, there weren't any.

Georgie Porgie, pudding and pie,
Kissed the girls and made them cry;
When the boys came out to play,
Georgie Porgie ran away.

Hey diddle, diddle,
The cat and the fiddle,
The cow jumped over the moon;
The little dog laughed
To see such sport,
And the dish ran away with the spoon.

Old Mother Hubbard
Went to the cupboard
To fetch her poor dog a bone;
But when she got there
The cupboard was bare,
And so the poor dog had none.

She went to the grocer's
To buy him some fruit;
But when she came back
He was playing the flute.

She went to the hatter's
To buy him a hat;
But when she came back
He was feeding the cat.

She went to the tailor's
To buy him a coat;
But when she came back
He was riding a goat.

The dame made a curtsey,
The dog made a bow;
The dame said, Your servant,
The dog said, Bow-wow.

Baa, baa, black sheep,
   Have you any wool?
Yes, sir, yes, sir,
   Three bags full;
One for my master,
   One for my dame,
And one for the little boy
   Who lives down the lane.

Polly, put the kettle on,   Sukey, take it off again,
Polly, put the kettle on,   Sukey, take it off again,
Polly, put the kettle on,   Sukey, take it off again,
   We'll all have tea.   They've all gone away.

Elsie Marley is grown so fine,
She won't get up to feed the swine,
But lies in bed till eight or nine,
    Lazy Elsie Marley.

Old Mother Goose,
   When she wanted to wander,
Would ride through the air
   On a very fine gander.

Rub-a-dub-dub,
Three men in a tub;
And who do you think they be?
The butcher, the baker,
The candlestick maker;
Turn 'em out, knaves all three!

To market, to market, to buy a fat pig,
Home again, home again, jiggety-jig;
To market, to market, to buy a fat hog,
Home again, home again, jiggety-jog.

Peter, Peter, pumpkin eater,
Had a wife and couldn't keep her;
He put her in a pumpkin shell
And there he kept her very well.

Sing a song of sixpence,
    A pocket full of rye;
Four and twenty blackbirds
    Baked in a pie!

When the pie was opened,
    The birds began to sing;
Wasn't that a dainty dish
    To set before the king?

The king was in his counting-house,
    Counting out his money;
The queen was in the parlor,
    Eating bread and honey.

The maid was in the garden,
    Hanging out the clothes;
There came a little blackbird,
    And snipped off her nose!

Barber, barber, shave a pig,
How many hairs to make a wig?
Four and twenty, that's enough.
Give the barber a pinch of snuff.

Peter Piper picked a peck of pickled peppers;
A peck of pickled peppers Peter Piper picked.
If Peter Piper picked a peck of pickled peppers,
Where's the peck of pickled peppers Peter Piper picked?

Jack Sprat could eat no fat,
His wife could eat no lean,
And so between them both, you see,
They licked the platter clean.

116

There was a jolly miller once,
    Lived on the river Dee;
He worked and sang from morn till night,
    No lark more blithe than he.

And this the burden of his song
    Forever used to be—
I care for nobody, no! not I,
    If nobody cares for me.

Old King Cole
Was a merry old soul,
And a merry old soul was he;
He called for his pipe,
And he called for his bowl,
And he called for his fiddlers three.

Every fiddler, he had a fine fiddle,
And a very fine fiddle had he;
Twee tweedle dee, tweedle dee, went the fiddlers.
Oh, there's none so rare
As can compare
With King Cole and his fiddlers three.

Fe, fi, fo, fum,
I smell the blood of an Englishman;
Be he alive or be he dead,
I'll grind his bones to make my bread.

Three little kittens,
They lost their mittens,
And they began to cry,
Oh, mother dear, we sadly fear
Our mittens we have lost.

What! Lost your mittens,
You naughty kittens!
Then you shall have no pie.
Mee-ow, mee-ow, mee-ow.
No, you shall have no pie.

The three little kittens,
They found their mittens,
And they began to cry,
Oh, mother dear, see here, see here
Our mittens we have found.

What! Found your mittens,
You silly kittens!
Then you shall have some pie.
Purr-r, purr-r, purr-r,
Oh, let us have some pie.

The three little kittens,
Put on their mittens,
And soon ate up the pie;
Oh, mother dear, we greatly fear
Our mittens we have soiled.

What! Soiled your mittens,
You naughty kittens!
Then they began to sigh,
Mee-ow, mee-ow, mee-ow.
Then they began to sigh.

The three little kittens,
They washed their mittens,
And hung them out to dry;
Oh, mother dear, look here, look here,
Our mittens we have washed.

What! Washed your mittens?
You're good little kittens.
But I smell a rat close by!
Hush! Hush! Hush!
I smell a rat close by.

The cat sat asleep by the side of the fire,
The mistress snored loud as a pig;
Jack took up his fiddle by Jenny's desire,
And struck up a bit of a jig.

Little maid, pretty maid, whither goest thou?
Down in the meadow to milk my cow.
Shall I go with thee? No, not now;
When I send for thee, then come thou.

One, two,
Buckle my shoe;

Three, four,
Knock at the door;

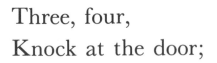

Five, six,
Pick up sticks;

128

Seven, eight,
Lay them straight;

Nine, ten,
A big fat hen.

A dillar, a dollar,
A ten-o'clock scholar,
What makes you come so soon?
You used to come at ten o'clock,
And now you come at noon.

Pussy cat, pussy cat, where have you been?
I've been to London to look at the queen.
Pussy cat, pussy cat, what did you there?
I frightened a little mouse under her chair.

Hector Protector was dressed all in green;
Hector Protector was sent to the queen.
   The queen did not like him,
   No more did the king;
So Hector Protector was sent back again.

Taffy was a Welshman,
　　Taffy was a thief,
Taffy came to my house
　　And stole a piece of beef.

I went to Taffy's house,
　　Taffy wasn't in,
I jumped upon his Sunday hat
　　And poked it with a pin.

Taffy was a Welshman,
　　Taffy was a sham,
Taffy came to my house
　　And stole a leg of lamb.

I went to Taffy's house,
    Taffy was away,
I stuffed his socks with sawdust
    And filled his shoes with clay.

Taffy was a Welshman,
    Taffy was a cheat,
Taffy came to my house
    And stole a piece of meat.

I went to Taffy's house,
    Taffy was in bed,
I took a marrow bone
    And beat him on the head.

137

Mistress Mary, quite contrary,
How does your garden grow?
With silver bells and cockle shells,
And pretty maids all in a row.

Little Miss Muffet
Sat on a tuffet,
Eating her curds and whey;
There came a big spider,
Who sat down beside her,
And frightened Miss Muffet away.

I had a little hen,
　　The prettiest ever seen;
She washed up the dishes,
　　And kept the house clean;
She went to the mill
　　To fetch me some flour,
And always got home
　　In less than an hour;

She baked me my bread,
   She brewed me my ale;
She sat by the fire
   And told a fine tale.

Blow, wind, blow! and go, mill, go!
That the miller may grind his corn;
    That the baker may take it,
    And into bread make it,
And bring us a loaf in the morn.

As I was going to St. Ives,
I met a man with seven wives.
Every wife had seven sacks,
Every sack had seven cats,
Every cat had seven kits;
Kits, cats, sacks, and wives,
How many were going to St. Ives?

Pussy cat, pussy cat,
    Wilt thou be mine?
Thou shalt not wash dishes
    Nor yet feed the swine,
But sit on a cushion
    And sew a fine seam
And feed upon strawberries,
    Sugar and cream.

Wee Willie Winkie runs through the town,
Upstairs and downstairs, in his nightgown;
Rapping at the window, crying through the lock,
Are the children all in bed, for now it's eight o'clock?

Star light, star bright,
First star I see tonight,
I wish I may, I wish I might,
Have the wish I wish tonight.

Good night,
Sleep tight,
Wake up bright
In the morning light,
To do what's right
With all your might.